1150

Teton Christmas Tales

By Betty Lemon
Illustrated by Phoebe Berrey

ISBN: 0-933160-06-2
Hardback

ISBN: 0-933160-07-0
Paperbound

Published
by
Teton Bookshop
Box 1903
Jackson, Wyoming 83001

For everyone, young or old, who believes in elves and sprites
and in the miracle of Christmas.

Giles and the Christmas Elf

In a small and remote mountain community there once lived a boy whose name was Giles. He was seven years old and rather small for his age. His parents and brothers and sisters lived in a large city, but because Giles was a frail boy, his grandmother and grandfather had asked him to live with them for a while where he could breathe good fresh mountain air and be out of doors much of the time. Giles sometimes grew a little lonely as he was too far from town to see much of the other children after school hours. He rode the school bus to and from school. There were no children his age who lived near, and his grandparents had not had a boy in their home for so long that at first they could not understand his loneliness and did not know how to talk to a boy in his own language. They always were kind to him, and they loved him very much, but they were too old to play his games with him and besides they were busy with their own work. So Giles began to invent games which he could play by himself. He loved to climb trees and imagine he was scaling the highest mountains. In the summer time he liked to make pets of the small animals that came to his grandparents' cabin, and he trained the chipmunks to eat from his hand and the mountain birds to lose their fear and fly low around him as he scattered crumbs for them. Occasionally he saw a doe with her fawn in the forest and wished he could get nearer to them and make friends. He built a crude little bird feeder, scattered seeds there in the winter, and was overjoyed when the first birds came to peck at the food. Soon others came, and Giles talked to them softly through the window as they ate. They learned that he would do them no harm, and soon looked up at him with their shiny black eyes and seemed to nod and talk to him, too.

Giles amused himself on rainy or snowy days by writing little verses. He liked words and the sound they made when spoken in rhythm. He liked to see if he could make words rhyme, and sometimes sang his childlike poems to himself as he walked in the meadows or in the forest. He moved softly and spoke gently, and all living creatures accepted him, knew no fear of him, considered him their friend, and seemed to understand his talking in poetry. Giles loved his grand-parents, but for his true companionship he turned to his animal and bird friends and to his little verses. Once he recited one of his poems to his grandparents as

1

they sat in the living room around the fire, but they did not seem to understand what he was trying to say, he became embarrassed, and wished he had kept his verse his own secret. Never again did he tell them of his poetry. He saved it rather for the creatures of the wood and stream and meadow who inspired most of it in his thoughts —

Poor little bird with injured wing,
I'll hold you close to me.
Soon you'll be well and then can fly
Happy and strong and free.

The chipmunk flicks his tail at me
There on a tree's gray limb.
He'll scamper to the ground, I know,
For nuts I hold for him.

In spite of Giles' desire to play with other children and have friends, he was usually a very happy boy. Often he wished his animal friends could speak to him and tell him of their adventures. But instead he would imagine what they had done and would talk to them about all they saw and did.

It was nearing Christmas time now, and many of Giles' bird friends had long since flown to warmer climates. Many of his animal friends had disappeared into some tree trunk or warm cave for the winter, and he knew he would not see them again until spring. So Giles began to feel his loneliness again and wished more than ever that he had someone with whom he could talk and to whom he could tell his little stories. He kept busy, though, and when school closed for the Christmas holiday, he helped his grandmother bake Christmas bread and cookies and fruit cakes. It was fun to decorate the cookies with colored frosting and to cut them into shapes of stars and gingerbread men and animals. He loved the spicy fragrance of the kitchen when his grandmother was baking. He loved to sample the various baked goods as they came hot from the oven, and he loved to "lick" the frosting bowls. In the evenings he enjoyed the huge fires his grandfather built in the fireplace, and he would sit before them and imagine stories about the red and orange and yellow flames that flickered over the enormous logs or occasionally he would see appearing through the smoke the wrinkled face of a tiny old man, and Giles would imagine who he was and from where he had come. On snowy mornings he would put on his snowshoes and walk over the sage flats near the cabin, and sometimes when the sun was setting, he would walk out again to see the last brilliant and rosy rays of the sun illuminating the clouds and the snow-capped peaks. He liked to look back at the tracks his snowshoes left in the snow and see how the shadows made each step clear and blue. In the winter evenings he would read the books he found on his grandparents' bookshelves; sometimes his grandfather would read to him and tell him how this story or that story had been a favorite of his father's when he was Giles' age.

One clear, cold day Giles and his grandfather took axe in hand and went to a nearby woods to choose a Christmas tree. They found a perfect one, not too big and not too small, one that had thick boughs and a fine, straight trunk. At first Giles did not like the idea of cutting the tree down. He feared it was the home of birds and squirrels and chipmunks in the summer time. But his grandfather explained to him that there were many others and that there were not many in the forest beautiful enough to be chosen for a boy's Christmas tree. This made Giles feel better. So home they went dragging the tree on a sled behind them. They set it up in a corner of the living room, and indeed the tree did look proud and happy to have been chosen for such an honor. The great box of Chirstmas decorations and ornaments was brought from the back of a closet, and the trimming began. Giles had a favorite ornament which he always put on the tree last of all, saving the best place on the green boughs for it. It was not the prettiest ornament, not even the brightest, but for some reason Giles loved it the best. It was round and red with silver stripes. Some of the red had chipped off, one or two of the silver stripes were tarnished, and his grandmother had suggested once that they throw it away for a prettier and newer one. But Giles held it tenderly in his hand and wanted to keep it. It seemed almost like a person to him. Sometimes when he held it to his ear, he thought he heard the sound of little bells or a tiny voice reciting a verse. Once he even imagined the song of a tiny mandolin came from it to him. So they kept the ornament, and Giles hung it high at the tip of one of the longest branches. The lights were lit when the tree was completely decorated, and the little boy and his grandparents stood off to admire it. Truly it was a lovely tree, and Giles' favorite ornament seemed to sing and wink at him in the glow of the lights. Giles said to himself a little verse about the ornament —

O little ornament of red,
Sweet peace and joy you send.
I love you best of all the rest.
You are my Christmas friend.

And the little ball kept nodding and sending joy to Giles in response to his verse.

On Christmas Eve the tree was lit, the grandparents and Giles had a fine supper of hot cakes and syrup before the big fire, the snow sparkled in the moonlight, and the stars above had never shone so bright and clear. The big turkey was ready to go into the oven early the next morning, the plum pudding had been baked, and Giles had helped cook the cranberry sauce, watching with delight as each berry popped its red shell and simmered low and fragrant in the rosy juice. After supper Giles went once more to admire his red and silver ornament, reached

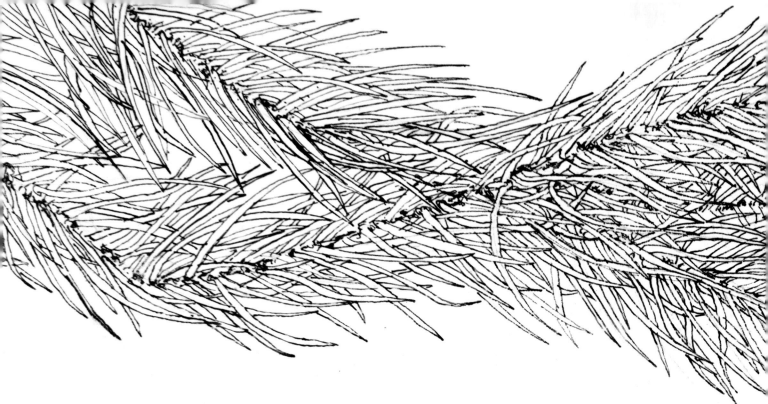

up to touch it with the tips of his fingers when all of a sudden it slipped from the bough and crashed to the floor below, splintering into a hundred bright slivers. Giles was horrified and grieved as he stooped to see the shattered ornament. He felt that it had been all his fault, his favorite decoration was gone forever and could never be replaced as no other ornament could ever be the same to him. No other ornament could he love so much. Tears came to his eyes and through them the bright shattered ornament became hazy and indistinct. Through the mist Giles suddenly heard a tiny voice, clear as a bell, saying to him, "Here I am, Giles. I had my home in your Christmas ornament. Now you have set me free, and I can talk to you and play with you." Giles looked down in wonder. There at his feet stood a tiny elf dressed in red with a small silver cap on his head and tiny silver bells on his red shoes. In his hand he held a tiny silver mandolin upon which he strummed as he spoke. Giles reached down and picked up the gay little fellow and held him in the palm of his hand. He smiled at his new friend and realized then why he had loved his red and silver ornament so much, why it had seemed like a person to him, why he had heard the sound of little bells and the playing of the tiny mandolin when he held the ornament close to his ear. The elf continued, "I have heard the little verses you speak. I write verses, too — listen!" And still strumming on the little mandolin, the elf spoke —

A little Christmas elf am I
And come to be with you.
We'll romp and play this Christmas time
And wondrous things we'll do.

4

We'll sing and dance and have gay times.
I'll show you joyous games.
We'll play with birds and mice and fawns,
I'll tell you all their names.

Such splendid stories I can tell
To please a little boy.
You'll be surprised at who I am —
I'm love and peace and joy.

So come with me and let me be
A Christmas friend to you.
I'll show you things you never dreamed.
We'll fashion verses, too.

And the little elf with one graceful leap jumped to the floor and beckoned Giles to follow him. He taught Giles to listen to the Christmas tree, and he heard a wonderful story of the things the tree had seen through all its long life, who had walked near its branches in the forest, what small animals had lived in its boughs and climbed its strong trunk. The Christmas elf on Christmas Day led Giles to the bird feeder and there taught him to understand what all the little creatures were saying to each other as they pecked the food. The elf perched on Giles' shoulder as he walked over the fields on his snowshoes, telling him of all that was sleeping under the snow, the small creatures, the flowers and shrubs. He always spoke in rhythm and played his tiny mandolin as he talked. Giles had never heard such marvelous tales nor had he ever played such wonderful games. His grandparents were pleased that he seemed so happy, that he looked so well, that he smiled so often. They were relieved, too, that he had not seemed to mind when his favorite Christmas ornament had broken. But Giles never told them his secret about the Christmas elf, and the little elf himself was careful to stay out of everyone's way and be seen only by his friend Giles.

The Christmas holidays soon drew to a close, and Giles knew he would have to return to school and that probably the little elf would disappear. On the last day of the vacation Giles and the elf had a particularly good time. The elf showed Giles where the chipmunks spent the winter, he showed him where the winter birds lived and pointed out in the snow the tracks of a marten. He showed him abandoned birds' nests, each with a cap of white snow now, like a tiny roof. He took Giles to a small hill near the river and showed him a family of young otters having a gay time sliding down the hill and romping with each other. In the evening as Giles was sitting sleepily and happily before the fire thinking over his wonderful Christmas holiday season, he felt a thistle-down weight on his shoulder, heard the tinkle of tiny bells, and the familiar strumming of the little mandolin. He knew the elf was there. He listened carefully and heard a whisper in his ear.

And now I'll leave you for a while,
Don't try to find my track.
We'll have more fun and happy times —
Next Chistmas I'll be back.
But in the meantime now and then,
If you will listen well,
You'll hear my voice in summer winds.
My stories I shall tell
In mountain streams and quiet lakes,
In pebbles round and bright,
In sunsets clear above the peaks,
In moon's and stars' white light.
On wings of birds you'll see me fly,
On chipmunks' backs I'll ride,
And you may hear my voice at night
In owl's mournful cry.
But you will have to pay close heed
If stories I may tell.
I only speak to those who hear —
And now, dear Giles — farewell!

Giles smiled and knew his friend would keep his promise. He said to himself but really more to his friend who he knew was listening —

I'm sure you'll come, I know you will,
Of that I'll never fear.
I'll listen well through all the year,
And hear you very near.

And then Giles heard a happy little song, the tiny strings of the little mandolin in the distance, and at last, thin and faint upon the cold, frosty air, the chime of joyous bells.

A Mouse Christmas

Once upon a time there was a family of mice. There were a mother and a father and three children, a girl, Amarintha, another girl, Arabella, and a boy, Timothy. Also in the family was an old grandmother who had come to live with her family when she decided that keeping her own house on the other side of the big meadow was getting to be too much work for her. Besides she was lonely and wanted the companionship of her family.

The mouse family lived in a large attic where they had found a comfortable home in an old mattress. There was a large family of people who lived downstairs. The mice, always interested in what was going on below them, would listen and peek through a large crack to watch the activities of the grown ups and children. Many times these activities seemed very strange to the mouse family, and sometimes the people said and did such amazing things that the mice upstairs would look at each other in wonder and astonishment. "How queer human beings are!" they thought.

Usually the mouse family was very happy, but sometimes life became dull and monotonous for them, and they wished for more excitement. The old granny felt that there was nothing much for her to do but sit and rock in her little mouse rocking chair. The father mouse had to go out every day to search for food for his family, and he felt that he would like to spend more time with his children. The mother mouse had so much to do to keep their mattress home clean and tidy and was so busy mending and cooking for her family that she became tired and did not laugh and joke the way she used to do. The children found time hanging heavily on their hands and often wished there was something exciting in their lives. These were the times when the little mouse family became sad. They felt that nothing they did was important. Even a little mouse must feel important if it wants to be happy.

One day the little mice were feeling especially depressed. It was cold out of doors, and in the afternoon large snowflakes began to fall. The skies were gray, and their mattress home seemed dull and gloomy. The children were huddled on the windowsill watching the snow fall. They wished they had something interesting to do. The old granny was rocking in her chair, nodding sleepily, her little

mouse spectacles dropping lower and lower on her long mouse nose. The mother was setting the table for dinner, and the father was bringing to the pantry some seeds and bread crumbs he had found. No one spoke. Everyone seemed sad. A mouse tear began to trickle down Timothy's furry little cheek. Suddenly Arabella saw something interesting out of doors. She looked again, and then called the others to come to see. The people downstairs had just driven to their door. With shouts and laughter, they were bringing into the house a big pine tree. "Come, look" Arabella cried. "See what is going on outside. The family is bringing a big tree into their house."

The little mouse family scampered to the window, and all peered out. Such goings on amazed them. "A tree in the house!" they all exclaimed. "Well, what next?" Tonight when the lights are lit, we'll peek through the crack and see what they are going to do with it."

The mice hurried with dinner, and the mother mouse quickly cleared away the dishes. Then each one took his place near the big crack to watch what was going on downstairs. The family stood the tree near a big window, and all members were gathered around to admire it. Then from little boxes they began to take out shiny balls and stars and hang them on the branches of the tree. There were strings of bright lights which were wound around the branches, too, and long silvery ribbons were hung from the tips. All the time the grown-ups and children danced gaily around the tree, talking and laughing happily. When the last box of ornaments had been opened and hung, they all stood back and shouted with joy. The tree was decorated and looked festive and twinkling especially when the tiny lights were lit.

The mouse family upstairs could hardly believe their eyes. Such a beautiful, beautiful tree! But what could this mean, bringing a tree indoors and decking it with such lovely, shiny trimmings? They looked enviously again and again at the tree. They could not take their shiny black mouse eyes from it, and suddenly Amarintha said, "Why can't we have a tree, too? Why can't we find decorations for it and trim it the way the people did?"

"Well, why not?" the father mouse said. "We don't know what it means, but it certainly is pretty, and a tree would look very nice in our living room. Tomorrow I'll go and find one."

"Oh, no, father," cried the mice children. "We want to go with you, it will be such fun!"

"Very well," said the father. "All of us will go early in the morning."

The little mice could hardly sleep that night because they were so eager for morning to come, but finally they drifted off to dreams of glittering trees and little mouse elves playing among the branches. The next morning they were awakened early by delicious smells from the kitchen. Their mother had planned a special treat and had a breakfast of hot pancakes and syrup, wee mouse pancakes, no bigger around than a thimble. Arabella ate seven, Amarintha ate nine, and Timothy ate twelve. Timothy had a slight stomach ache later in the morning, but he didn't tell anyone, and soon it went away. Then the mouse family put on their caps and coats, even old granny, and all started off to look for a tree. On the top of the snow they left behind them the tracks of twenty-four tiny mouse feet, and between these ran a long, thin mark where six mouse tails had followed behind. At last, after looking long and hard, they found buried in the snow exactly the tree they wanted. And this is a secret — it wasn't really a tree at all, but a beautifully shaped pine cone, just right to be decorated for a mouse family.

They lifted it gently, and carried it home, laughing and talking all the way.

They propped it in the corner, and such joyful mouse shrieks and cries you couldn't imagine. Then the whole family began the search for ornaments. The children scampered one way, the granny another, and the mother and father still another, and soon all returned with lovely trimmings. There were scraps of bright paper, shiny tinsel, several bright beads which someone had found in an old box, and little Timothy even found a tiny gold star which someone in the family downstairs had once used for a pin. Then everyone, even the old granny, began to trim the tree, and if you thought the shouting and happiness downstairs the night before had been joyous, you should have heard the mouse cries and shouts of glee upstairs — that was the best of all. When the little tree had been completely decorated, the mice joined hands and danced around it, their bright eyes shining and their tails thumping the floor excitedly. All day long the eyes of the mouse family wandered to their tree which they thought the prettiest thing they had ever seen in their whole lives.

That night the mouse family again collected by the big crack, and twelve bright mouse eyes watched again what was happening downstairs. This was even more wonderful than the night before had been. Each member of the family was in a corner, and each was wrapping in red and green and silver and blue and gold paper big boxes, little boxes, medium-sized boxes. One of the people said, "I know she will like my present." Another said, "I know he will like mine because he has wanted one for a long, long time." A third said, "My present to her will be the nicest of all because I made it myself."

"Presents?" the mouse family thought. "What are presents? They sound very nice." "I know what presents are," said the old granny. "I remember now. I learned about them in a big house where I lived when I was a little girl. They are things you give to those you love, things they want and will like. Surprises they sometimes call them."

"How wonderful!" the little mice cried. "We want presents and surprises, too. Let's all find pretty things to give to each other."

The mouse parents and granny agreed, and for the next few days in the attic there was a hurrying and scurrying such as only a mouse family can make. Each one searched and searched through the attic, each one worked and worked on his presents to make them the loveliest of all, and at night Timothy, because he was the smallest and could get in and out of tiny cracks the easiest, was sent down in the dark to pick up scraps of bright paper and ribbons which the people had not wanted and had thrown away. When he returned with his little mouse arms full of gay wrappings, each one of his family took some and began to wrap his presents. There were stacks and stacks of them, and the mice, like the people, put each one under the bright tree. After all had been finished, the mother mouse announced that she had a surprise for all of them. She brought out two rose hips apiece

which all ate with great relish, particularly the little black seeds as mice love seeds better than anything in the world. Then the mother passed a big bowl of mouse popcorn, and all sat around the tree with the heaps of presents under the branches and had a family mouse party. All were happy and excited. All felt very important.

Suddenly from downstairs the little mice heard music. Someone was singing a lovely song, and then a whole chorus joined in the singing of another. Song after song, beautiful songs, rose in the air, and the mouse family, all gathered now around their crack, thought they were the most wondrous sounds they ever had heard. Before long, the little mice began humming along with the music, granny in her high cracked voice, the children in their strong little mouse voices. They did not really know what they were humming or singing, but it was beautiful anyway, all about joy coming to the world, a beautiful star, something wonderful that happened in a manger, angels' singing, and a little town somewhere called Bethlehem. The little mouse family looked at each other with joy in their eyes as they drew closer together in the dark and continued their soft singing, thumping their little mouse tails rhythmically to keep time.

After the singing downstairs had stopped, the little mice heard the father of the family reading from a large, black book these words:

And there were in the same country shepherds abiding in the field, keeping watch over their flock by night. And, lo, the angel of the Lord came upon them, and the glory of the Lord shone round about them: and they were sore afraid. And the angel said unto them, Fear not: for, behold, I bring you good tidings of great joy, which shall be to all people. For unto you is born this day in the city of David a Saviour, which is Christ the Lord. And this shall be a sign unto you; Ye shall find the babe wrapped in swaddling clothes, lying in a manger. And suddenly there was with the angel a multitude of the heavenly host praising God, and saying,
Glory to God in the highest, and on earth peace, good will toward men.

And it was then that the little mouse family began to understand. All the mysteries of the past days slowly became clear to them. They knew now why gifts were given and why there was singing about a child in a manger, angels, and the unbounded joy which was promised to all. The mice looked at each other and smiled. "Even for a tiny family like ours," granny said, "love and kindness and understanding are possible because of the Child who was born in a manger years ago. Now we know what all the celebration means. We understand it and can feel it in our hearts." All the others nodded their heads because they understood, too, and when they went to sleep that night, their hearts were filled with love and joy. They dreamed of the Christ Child who was born to bring goodness to all creatures.

The next morning the people downstairs opened their presents and were happy and pleased with all they received. The little mice wanted to do the same, so they hurried with their breakfasts and morning chores. Arabella dried the dishes — she had never offered to help before, but found it made her feel happy to work with her mother, and her mother was pleased. She cracked one plate, but her mother didn't scold her as she was trying so hard. Amarintha dusted the living room so it would be tidy for the opening of presents. She forgot to dust under one table and two chairs, but nobody cared since she wanted so much to be helpful. Timothy made the beds and left them lumpy, but the others only laughed and thought his attempts to be useful were quite wonderful. The mouse children all enjoyed doing their chores and felt very important. Then the opening of the presents began, and such an array you have never seen. Knit socks and caps and mittens from granny whose knitting needles had been clicking furiously for the past few days. There was a new shawl for granny herself and a pair of slippers lined with milkweed down to keep her mouse feet warm. There were gloves lined with soft bird feathers for the mother and father. There were little mouse dolls with lovely big ears and pointed noses for Arabella and Amarintha. The father had carved these from chips of wood and also a handsome wooden truck for Timothy. Each mouse child got a pair of tiny skis which the father mouse had cut from curved twigs, smoothed, and painted in bright colors. It was a lovely day for the entire mouse family. Each felt happier than he had ever felt in his life because each felt a part of the family and very important to have found such lovely presents for the others. Each thought to himself that he would never feel bored again since each had found how exciting and how much fun it is to work and plan and play together. And all through their happy thoughts they remembered the Child in the manger and understood it was really He who had brought true joy and love to the world. That night before they went to bed, all the little mice joined in the singing which was again coming from downstairs. Every heart in that big house was full of joy and happiness, the mouse hearts not the least.

If you have a big attic, listen about this time of year for a faint scratching and scrambling above you. If you hear it, it may be another mouse family working and playing together in their plans for joyous and happy days of trees and ornaments and presents and singing. And if you listen very carefully while carols are being sung, you may even hear the little mouse family joining in, gently thumping their little mouse tails to keep time.

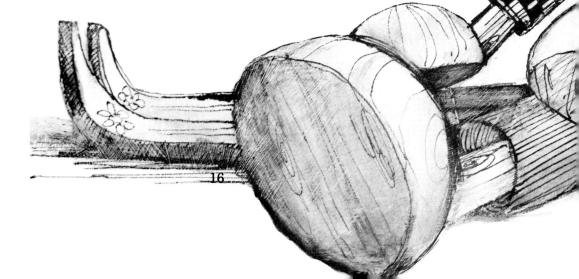

The Greatest Gift of All

On a small ranch in a high and mountainous area in the West lived an elderly couple. This couple had spent their childhood in Denmark, but after they were married, they heard about the beauties and opportunities in a new country and had come to live here permanently. They had chosen their particular ranch as the most beautiful spot they had ever seen and were glad to be able to raise their son in such lovely surroundings. Now that their son had married and had gone to live in a city, the couple spent their time with chores on the ranch, enjoying their quiet and peaceful life. They found their later years happy and satisfying. Their son came to visit them often, and always they looked forward to his visits with great pleasure. He brought his wife with him and his son named Kent. The three visitors from the city enjoyed to the full the time spent on the ranch, but most of all they liked being with the two grandparents who found so much joy in having the family together.

The young father and mother and their eight-year-old son Kent had not visited the ranch for several months, and they all were eager to go back where the air was fresh and pure, where there were wide open spaces inhabited by wild animals and birds, where for a brief period of time they could escape the noise and soot and bustle of city living. Kent was eager to see the ranch again and especially his grandparents whom he loved dearly. "When are we going back to the ranch?" he often asked his parents. "When are we going to see grandma and grandpa again?" But there were many things which had to be done in the city and there never seemed to be just the right time to take a vacation long enough for a visit to the ranch. One day, however, a letter from the grandparents came, inviting and urging the family to spend Chirstmas with them. It was early November when the letter arrived, and at once the family decided to go. Things in the city could wait. All of them were ready for a peaceful, happy vacation in the mountains. So plans were made, suitcases were packed, and immediately after Thanksgiving the family left their city home and headed for the ranch. The thought of a whole month of quiet and freedom made their hearts light and their spirits gay.

When they arrived at the ranch, there was a fine welcome for them. The grandparents were delighted to see their family again, and Kent and his parents were just as happy to be there. The ranch house was filled with merry talk and laughter. Kent raced from one place to another to be certain that nothing had changed. He saw the cattle, visited the horses, and was pleased when he caught glimpses of an enormous moose wandering over the sage flats. He listened to the songs of the chickadees as they came to the bird feeder, he admired the beauty of the big blue jays as they pecked for seeds on the snowy ground. He was happy to see his old friends, the pine squirrel and weasel, as they snatched chunks of suet off the feeder. He thought that never would he get his fill of this beautiful country even if he lived to be a thousand years old. The clean white snow sparkled in the sunlight and again by the light of the moon. The pine trees stood tall and stately, their thick branches covered with snow until the lower ones were bent to the ground. Every morning when Kent was eating his hearty breakfast in the warm ranch kitchen, he saw that every twig of every tree and bush was covered with white frost feathers. He loved to hear a gentle wind stirring the branches of the trees and bushes; he loved to see the light frost blown away, filling the air with multi-colored sparkles.

On the morning of December first, Kent's grandparents said they had a surprise for him. They showed him a gay tapestry on the wall which they said had been made many years before in Denmark. On the tapestry were brightly dressed elves, twenty-four of them, and pinned to the hand of each was a tiny slip of paper. Kent was going to carry on an old Danish tradition which his grandparents had known when they were children. Each day from the first of December until the twenty-fourth Kent was to open one of the slips of paper and follow its instruction. His eyes became wide at the thought and he was eager to begin the old Danish Christmas game at once. So he went to the first slip of paper, opened it, and read, "Go look on the third pantry shelf." Kent ran directly to the place and there he found a gaily wrapped package. He quickly opened it and found inside a pair of warm woolen mittens which his grandmother had knit for him. He exclaimed with happiness and immediately put them on. They fit perfectly. From then on, each day Kent drew one of the slips of paper which the elves held, followed its directions were to look, and always he found a gift wrapped and ready for him to open. There were toys, books, things to wear like caps and socks, there were candies and nuts and fruits, each little gift even better than the last. His grandparents, however, told him to wait. The last gift was to be the best of all and he would surely love that one the most.

In the meantime, as Kent was opening and enjoying each gift every day, the grown-ups were busy preparing for Christmas Eve and Christmas Day itself. The men found a fine Christmas tree in the nearby forest. They brought it to the living room where all the decorations were laid — shiny Christmas balls, glistening tinsel, bright stars, tiny birds. There were wrapped gifts for everyone laid under the tree. Big logs were brought in to keep the fires in the fireplace burning brightly. The grandmother and Kent's mother were busy in the kitchen most of the time. The most wonderful fragrances came from their cooking of all kinds of cookies, plum puddings, pies. Finally the big turkey was ready to be stuffed with its dressing and put into the oven.

The day before Christmas arrived and Kent, remembering that the last gift of the elves was to be the best of all, was eager to find and open it. But his grandparents told him that this time he must wait until after their Christmas Eve dinner to open the gift. The day seemed long to Kent and he was impatient for evening to arrive. He noticed that his grandfather had pulled down one shade in the living room just before dinner. He wondered if this had something to do with the last and best gift, but he asked no questions. Soon another big log was thrown onto the fire, the lights on the Christmas tree were lit, and the family sat down to their Christmas Eve supper of steaming hot oyster stew, home made golden brown rolls, fruit cake and Danish pastries. Everyone seemed to eat so annoyingly slowly, Kent thought, but it was not long before all had finished, the dishes were cleared away, and Kent knew that now at last was the time for the finest gift of all from the elves. As he went to get the last slip of instructions from the tapestry, his grandfather turned out the lights. The room was lit only by the Christmas tree lights and the glow from the fireplace. By this dim light Kent read the final instructions, "Go to the living room window and raise the shade." Quietly and slowly he moved across the room, stopped at the window, and with excited, trembling fingers gently raised the shade. He looked out upon the old familiar scene which he loved so much, the wide expanse of sage flats, the snowy mountains rising in the distance, the dark pine trees. The snow sparkled and glistened, the stars had never seemed so close. The cold, silver moon was just rising, casting its light on the river beyond. For a moment Kent said nothing. He though, "A present? How can this be a present, the finest and best of all?" And then he heard a light, sweet voice on his shoulder. He looked down and there was a sprightly elf who whispered in his ear. "Yes, Kent, this is the finest gift of all. Look out. See the mountains. See the river and the sage flats. See the tall, dark pines with snow-laden branches. Look up at the moon and the stars. See how they are looking down at you and how they make the snow twinkle with a million bright diamonds. This is yours to love and remember always. If you are lucky, maybe some day you will return here to live forever." And the little voice stopped. The elf disappeared from Kent's shoulder.

Kent gave a long look — up, down, and around, and then he thought to himself, "Yes, this is the finest gift of them all. Nothing in the world could be greater

than this." With shining eyes he turned to look at his grandparents and parents who stood near. He stretched out his arms to them as they stooped to hug him tight and close. They could tell by his happy expression that he understood.

The Sprite's
Magic Flute

Many, many years ago there was a tiny village situated high on the slope of a mighty mountain. There was a church and a school, a store or two, and the neat little homes all bordered the only road which led through the village. It was a happy place, and the adults and children alike loved their village and all the mountain meadows and streams and lakes and forests which surrounded it. Gay voices of the children could be heard often as there were many out of door excursions, up to the mountain meadows where there were wild flowers to pick, down to the mountain streams, into the forests where there were berries and nuts. The grown up people were happy, too, and they went about their work with contentment and satisfaction. Occasionally visitors from distant parts came to the village to see the beautiful scenery or to buy some of the clever handiwork which was made there, but usually there was no one except the villagers themselves who lived quiet, peaceful lives with little contact with the outside world.

Only one thing saddened and disturbed the little group of villagers — there were no birds anywhere near them. No sweet songs in the early spring, no bird notes all summer long, none in the fall or winter. At one time there had been a few birds, but these had strangely disappeared. No one knew why. Perhaps the winters were too cold to attract snow birds, perhaps the village was too high on the mountain — whatever the reason, no one had seen a bird flying over the creeks, no one had seen a bird building a nest in the trees, no one had heard the sound of a bird's singing for many years. Some of the men had gone to the low lands for the express purpose of bringing birds back with them. They had returned with cages full of birds which they immediately had released. The birds had looked around and then just as quickly taken flight back down the side of the mountain to return to their familiar surroundings in other forests, in other meadows. You won't believe it, but some of the children and young people in the village had never seen a bird or heard it sing. Have you ever thought what it would be never to have seen a bird or heard its sweet song? It was sad indeed, and the villagers could not imagine what the trouble was.

Finally it worried and saddened the people so deeply that they thought they would do anything to bring birds to their village. Groups of adults and children

26

started out and roamed over the meadows and through the forests searching, always searching to see if some one of them could find a hidden nest somewhere, catch sight of a bird in the tree tops, come upon a broken egg on the ground. Never a thing did they find, and always they returned to their homes more troubled than ever. Finally the people sent word to all the villages in the low lands, promising a reward if anyone could bring birds to them. Several volunteers, eager for the reward, came and tried all kinds of things to bring birds, but none of them was successful. The meadows, the lakes, the forests remained as silent as always.

It was early winter. All of the meadow flowers had withered and gone to seed. Ice was beginning to form on the lakes, and once or twice dark clouds hung heavy over the village and sent down brief showers of snow. The days grew shorter, the nights colder, and as Christmas approached, there were many plans made for the usual holiday festivities. Women in their kitchens prepared Christmas geese and turkeys, the fragrance of fresh plum pudding pervaded the homes, men went into the forest to choose Christmas trees, and the children grew wide-eyed and excited when they saw mysterious packages brought into the house, wrapped, and hidden away until Christmas morning.

On Christmas Eve when the lights were just beginning to show through the windows of the homes and the fires were being lighted, a strange thing happened. A tiny spark of light appeared at the end of the village road. It shone and twinkled in the moonlight and moved forward. It danced gaily as it advanced and sometimes seemed to rise into the air, float there for a second, and then return to the ground. As it came nearer, shades in the houses were raised, windows were thrown open that the people might see more clearly what was coming. They saw a figure no taller than two feet, a pointed cap on its head, and small pointed ears showing from under the cap. The small sprite was dressed in a long gray cloak with streaks of black through it and a touch of white at the throat. He looked neither to the right nor the left as he danced along. Suddenly he drew something from underneath his cloak, lifted it to his lips where it shone silvery and bright in the light of the moon. What the little creature held was a flute, and from it came the sweetest sounds the villagers had ever heard. All the people were enchanted by the beautiful music.

They put on their wraps and opened their doors to go out so that they might see the tiny cloaked figure better, might hear the songs more distinctly. The sprite moved slowly and the villagers could see it more clearly. They saw that its peaked cap was black and covered with hundreds of tiny shining stars. They saw that the sprite had a merry, laughing face and sparkling, kind eyes. The people began to follow it silently and timidly. At the end of the road, the sprite turned and moved back, walking with feather-light steps, still playing the wonderful music on the silver flute. All the people were silent, afraid the lovely sounds would cease, the figure disappear. But on and on it walked, always playing the magic music. And then the sprite began to speak, and all held their breath to be sure to catch every word. "You want birds in your village," the musical voice said. "You shall have birds as my Christmas gift to you. But I must have my reward which you promised. My reward shall be that always you will treat my birds kindly and take them to your hearts. Leave crumbs and seeds on your window sills for them, talk to them gently, and they will learn to trust you and love you." All of the villagers, amazed and wondering, nodded their heads in understanding and softly murmured, "Yes, yes. We will do all that. We shall love the birds and make them know we are their friends and that this is their village, too."

And with that the sprite lifted his flute to his lips again. From the flute came the most beautiful song yet, sweet, cheerful, friendly. And — would you believe it? — as the villagers watched the flute with fascination, they could actually see the notes dancing forth. Small they were at first, then they seemed to grow larger as they floated into the cold, still air. The eyes of the villagers left the sprite and watched with wonder the notes as they came faster and faster. And then each note turned silvery gray with black designs through it, exactly like the cloak of the musician. Each note, like a miracle, became a tiny bird, soft and feathery. Finally the music of the flute stopped, but even sweeter sounds took its place. The throat of each tiny bird trembled slightly, and then the air was filled with the most glorious notes of all, the singing of birds which surpasses all other sounds in the world. On and on the birds sang, on and on they flew above the heads of the villagers, some lighting on the shoulders of the children, some on their out-stretched hands. Chick-a-dee-dee-dee the birds sang over and over until the villagers burst into delighted shouts and began to sing their own songs with the little birds. But when the people looked back at the place where the sprite had been standing, he had vanished. Not a sign or trace of him at all. But the birds continued to fly about and sing. They followed the villagers as they slowly turned homeward.

And that night not a window sill in the whole village but was covered with a generous supply of crumbs and seeds. And on Christmas morning as soon as the sun touched the roofs of the houses, the trees white with snow, not a window sill in the whole village that was not visited by dozens of tiny gray and black birds with a touch of white at their throats. The finest Christmas gift that had ever been received, all agreed. The sight of the graceful birds in the trees, the sounds of their beautiful songs through the entire village — chick-a-dee-dee-dee — con-tinued there forever to bring cheer and happiness to all the people and to remind them of their Christmas gift bestowed by the friendly little sprite of a musician who had visited them so miraculously on that wondrous Christmas Eve.

Granny's Cuckoo Clock

In a far distant mountain area, there was a tiny village populated by happy, industrious people who loved their homes and beautiful surroundings. The adults enjoyed their work on ranches and in small businesses in town. The children played together and studied together in school with happiness and pleasure. Gay sounds rang from the streets and meadows and forests when the children were not at school, and many were the good times the children and adults had together on holidays and festive occasions.

One of the neat little homes in the village was occupied by an elderly lady who lived all alone. In the summer months she kept busy during the day in her garden, and in winter months she loved to spend time in her kitchen baking and in her tiny living room sewing and knitting. After school many children stopped by to see her, for they loved Granny, as they all called her, very much. She always invited them in to have a freshly baked cookie or two or a little honey cake which her young friends particularly liked. The children stopped a while and visited with Granny, told her about their day at school, what they were going to do now that school was over for the day, and all their plans for the coming days. Granny was always interested to hear their tales and looked forward all day to seeing the children headed her way, eager to talk with her and to listen, too, to what she had been doing all day while they had been in school. On weekends she had frequent visitors among the children. Many adults, too, stopped to see her and share cookies, cakes, and hot tea with her. She was never lonely during the days, as work in her house or garden kept her busy, but sometimes at night Granny felt very lonely and missed the gay talk and laughter of the day. Her home was very quiet then. Not a sound could be heard. The evening hours after dinner were sad and long. Granny took up her knitting then, hummed a little tune to herself, but it was usually a sad little tune and did not help to make her happier. Sometimes on pleasant evenings she would put on her shawl and bonnet and take a short walk, but these walks did not help much either. She passed the lighted homes of her neighbors and heard from within the shouts and laughter of her friends. These walks really made her feel more lonesome and alone, so soon she returned to her own home where it was silent with no sound at all in any room.

Granny dreaded the Christmas holiday more than any other time. Her friends were very kind to her, and the children trooped in often during the holiday season and often brought her samples of what their mothers were baking in their kitchens. Granny enjoyed the fruit cakes, the plum pudding, the roast goose which the children brought her, but still it was a lonely season for her and her house in the evenings seemed very quiet, much more so than usual.

One of the children who loved Granny best was an eight-year-old boy named Jeremy. He sensed her loneliness and told his mother and father about it. "Granny seems happy during the day, and she always enjoys having us visit her and talk with her, but I think she must be very lonely at night. Her house must be quiet when all of us go home. I wish there were something we could do to help her and make her evenings less lonesome." Jeremy's mother and father agreed, although they had not thought of it before, and decided that something must be done so that Granny's home would be less silent when all her friends had gone. They thought and thought and finally it was Jeremy who had the best idea. "I know what let's do! Let's get Granny a cuckoo clock that will keep her company. The cuckoo will pop out of its house every few minutes and greet her and be her friend." Jeremy's parents thought that this was a wonderful idea. The father, who happened to be a skilled cabinet maker, said that he himself would make the clock. They would present it to Granny just before Christmas. It was to be kept a deep secret and a real surprise.

The very next day the father gathered together in his shop all the materials he would need, the wood for the clock itself, the heavy weights, the chains for them, the paint he would use to decorate the clock, and last of all the material he would need to make the tiny cuckoo which would be Granny's friend and help to make her evenings happy. After school Jeremy stopped at his father's shop and looked admiringly at all the things that were ready. He begged to be allowed to help, so his father promised to permit him to do the simple jobs. Jeremy then could feel that he, too, had had a part in making Granny's present.

In a few days the clock was finished and how handsome it was! It worked beautifully, the weights of the chains, the small door of the cuckoo's house which sprang open and let the bird pop out and sing its cheerful song. The clock kept accurate time, too. It was the finest cuckoo clock in the world.

The day before Christmas arrived and Jeremy's mother invited Granny to come to their home in the afternoon to have fruit cake and tea. This was done so that Jeremy and his father could take the cuckoo clock to Granny's house while she was away, find a suitable place for it, and have it ready for her when she returned. Jeremy and his father tiptoed into Granny's house, looked around, found just the right place to hang the clock, and then carefully, oh so carefully, lifted it and hung it in place. They made sure that everything was right, waited a few minutes until it was time for the cuckoo to appear, and when they saw that all worked well, out they tiptoed, closed the door softly behind them, and went

home, just in time to find Granny ready to leave. When she left, Jeremy, his mother, and father followed her without her realizing it. When she went into her home, there were three excited faces looking in the window to watch her surprise when she first saw the clock and heard the cuckoo sing. They were not disappointed — it was the first thing Granny saw when she went into the room. Her twinkling eyes opened wide, she clasped her hands, and looked with wonder and admiration at the beautiful new clock. Its tick-tock, tick-tock sounded gay, and when the cuckoo appeared and greeted her, Granny laughed aloud with happiness. At that moment the three people watching from the outside of the house, burst in, and all joined hands and danced in a circle in front of the clock. There where tears of joy in Granny's eyes, and perhaps in the eyes of the three who had given her such a fine Christmas gift.

After her supper that night, Granny sat dozing in front of her fire. There was a smile on her lips as she remembered her lovely new clock. She dropped off to sleep for a minute, and in that minute the strangest thing happened that you ever did hear. Suddenly there was the sound of a creak from one part of the room, a scampering from another part, and a merry chuckle from still another. From all parts of the room appeared the queerest little creatures that you could possibly imagine. Elves they were, dressed all in red and green, and they, too, saw the new clock and were fascinated by it. Up the heavy weights they swung, up the chains, onto the roof of the cuckoo's house itself, and when the bird appeared to see what was going on they shouted with delight. Up and down the elves scampered and climbed, examining every inch of the clock.

And then on that happiest of all of Granny's Christmas Eves, the elves disappeared. Not a sign of them was left, not a note of their magic songs could be heard. Granny stirred a little in her sleep, then awoke just as the cuckoo appeared again at the door of its house and sang out "Cuckoo! Cuckoo!" which sounded to Granny remarkably like "Merry Christmas!" She looked at the bird, gently waved to it as it disappeared into its house, and for some reason or other she felt happier than she had in a long, long time. It seemed that her lonely evenings had all vanished now that she had the little bird to keep her company, the soft tick-tock of the clock to break the silence in her house. And could it be — she smiled to herself at the very idea — but somehow she seemed to hear tiny, silvery voices from all parts of the room which joined together at last in a strange little song which amused Granny immensely —

So this is Granny's cuckoo clock,
A Christmas gift from friends.
We'll add a touch of magic
Before this story ends.
We'll whisper spells and elfin charms
Into the cuckoo's ear

So every time he sings his song
For Granny waiting near,
He'll bring her love and happiness
With each tick-tock, tick-tock.
Her days and nights, all filled with joy.
It's now a magic clock!

Mareth's Gift

A long time ago, there lived in a far distant land a little girl and her family. The little girl's name was Mareth. She had no brothers or sisters, there were few children who lived near, so she found her greatest happiness in the animals who grazed on the sparse feed around her home, and in rainy, cold weather slept in her father's stable. She had many animals, a pretty white and brown calf, a snow white lamb, a newborn colt, but her favorite of all was a baby burro whom she named Tallah. Tallah was soft gray, had long fuzzy ears, and the most beautiful kind eyes you could imagine. Her curly coat was unmarked, and only her ears and her tiny hooves were black. Tallah was just a few weeks old, but she was a lively little burro and scampered around the stable and followed Mareth everywhere she went, prancing and dancing at her side. Burros, Mareth knew, live to be very, very old, so she was pleased to think that she would have Tallah to love and keep as her very own for many, many years.

Mareth sometimes wished she had brothers and sisters to play with, and often she grew lonely when her father and mother were busy tending their inn. Many people came to the inn and there never was lack of company, but usually the guests were grown-ups who talked about business, their crops and stock, and these things did not interest Mareth. Once in a while a child came with his parents to the inn, but no sooner did Mareth become acquainted with the child than he had to move on with his family. When she felt lonely, she busied herself feeding her animals or giving them fresh water from the well. Sometimes she would take long walks, and then she wanted only Tallah with her. She would speak to Tallah of all they saw on their walks, showing Tallah a pretty flower here, a scampering rabbit there, and she would also tell Tallah of all her loneliness, her dreams, her desire for children who could be her friends. Tallah seemed to understand all she said, would listen with her long ears pricked forward, would look at Mareth with kindly, sympathetic eyes. Sometimes Mareth would weave wreaths of flowers and adorn Tallah's little head with them. When Tallah raced and bucked, her flower wreath bobbing up and down, Mareth would laugh gaily, her black eyes sparkling, her red lips parted in joy. At these times Mareth was happy and did not want any other companion but Tallah.

It was mid winter, and people were coming from the distant countryside to Mareth's village to pay their yearly taxes. The inn where Mareth lived was filled with people, and they seemed comfortable by the warm fire as the wind was chill outdoors. Mareth thought contentedly of her little animals in the stable where they were warm and well protected. Once she slipped out of the inn and went to the stable where she searched for Tallah. Mareth ran her slim brown fingers under Tallah's heavy coat and was comforted to find it warm. As she went back to the inn, she noticed two people approaching, probably, she thought, to find room and shelter for the night. Mareth knew there was no room and wondered what these tired, cold people would do as there was no other place for them to go. As she went into the side door of the inn, the man and woman were entering the front door. She heard them inquire for lodging, and then heard her father say there was no room. Mareth thought of the comfortable, warm stable, the clean, dry straw which could serve for a bed, and she went to her father to make this suggestion. Her father looked down at her, smiled, and then made the offer of his stable which the man and woman, tired and worn as they were, accepted at once.

Mareth ran back to the stable, heaped armsful of straw in one corner, put each animal into its stall, and when the couple came, things were ready for them. Mareth lit an old oil lamp and took it to them with a bowl of food which had been left over from the suppers of the other guests. She gave Tallah one last pat and hug as she passed her stall, and then went to her own bed for the night.

She was sleeping soundly and sweetly when suddenly she was awakened by a bright light, full of splendor and glory. She went to the window and looked up to the heavens and saw something that made her so frightened at first that she drew back. But as soon as her eyes had become accustomed to the brilliance, she crept back to the window to watch. It was a star, larger and more beautiful than any star she had ever seen, and it was shining directly above her father's stable. She sat for a long time looking at the star, wondering from where it had come and what it meant. Then she became aware of people moving about in the courtyard below, and over and above everything else there was a mysterious, wondrous light from the star. She saw her father and mother hurrying to the stable, she saw shepherds coming with their long crooks, and then, a little later, like a wonderful dream, she saw riding into the courtyard on three camels, three strange men dressed in silks and velvets, each carrying a jeweled box. Mareth could endure the excitement no longer, so she hurriedly got dressed, and she, too, ran to the courtyard to see what was happening. Something strange and magic filled the air, something like the fragrances of spring, the songs of birds, the love she felt for her mother and father, for Tallah. Strains of mystic music, like the singing of an angel chorus, fell upon her ears. She thought she had never felt anything so joyous in her whole life.

She approached the stable which by this time was filled with people, crept around the edge, and peered in to see the sight which held all the people, shep-

41

herds and wise men alike, in such silent awe. Her eyes dropped, and there she saw again the man and woman whom she had led to the stable, and between them, wrapped in swaddling clothes, was a tiny baby, beautiful beyond words, and all around Him shone a heavenly light. Mareth moved closer and saw that the people were laying gifts at the baby's feet, frankincense, myrrh, jewels. Mareth's eyes opened wide at the magnificent sight. But the most miraculous thing of all was the baby, and she watched Him, feeling an overwhelming love fill her soul, a desire to adore and follow Him always. What could she give the baby? What did she have that would make Him happy? She knew of nothing, she could think of nothing worthy of such a marvelous baby with the splendor of heaven shining about Him. Her heart grew sad. She, too, wanted to give to this Child. And then — her eyes fell upon Tallah. How she loved Tallah! How she felt joy in all they did together and talked about together. How she would miss Tallah, and what loneliness she would feel without her. But this was her loveliest possession. Tallah was a baby and surely the new baby lying there in the straw would love Tallah, too. Quietly she went to Tallah, stroked her long ears, patted her neck, and then throwing a halter over her head, she led her toward the new baby. She put the end of the rope into the mother's hand and said, "Here, take Tallah. This is my gift to the new baby." The mother smiled at Mareth, the baby looked up and seemed to smile, too, and suddenly the light which surrounded the baby shone briefly on Mareth's face as she moved back into the shadows.

Many years passed. Mareth grew into a slim, beautiful girl with the same dark hair about her face, the same black eyes, the same laughing mouth. She continued to love and care for her animals, and she often thought tenderly of her favorite of them all, the little burro Tallah, and wondered what had happened to her and if the baby, now a grown man, loved her and took good care of her. Mareth finally married a good man, and they went to live in a home of their own. They had children who played happily around the house and who, like their mother, loved all the animals they had. Somewhere in the crowd of animals was always a burro or two, gay little creatures who found life joyful, but never was there one so beautiful and companionable as Tallah had been. Mareth often saw Tallah in her dreams, a mature Tallah now, but still with the same soft eyes, the long furry ears. Mareth though she had never missed anything in her life so much as she missed Tallah. She longed to see her, at least to know that wherever she was, she was safe and happy.

One sunny spring day, Mareth was sitting under a large, shady tree in the yard of her home. She was enjoying the warm sun, the soft breezes, the fragrance of the flowers, the songs of the birds. She had a strange feeling that somewhere before she had experienced this same peace, joy, contentment. She knew that sometime earlier in her life, there had been this precise feeling of love which flooded her heart, love for the flowers, love for the soft air, love for the animals she saw around her, love for her family, love for all humanity. And suddenly she

recognized the feeling. It was the same she had felt in the stable many years before when she had seen the baby lying on the straw and had given Him Tallah as her most precious gift.

As she was sitting musing, she noticed coming up the road a man who was leading something behind him. Mareth rose from her seat, shaded her eyes with her hand, and felt a quickening of her heart beat, her breath coming short. The man approached, stopped at the gate, and then Mareth noticed that he was leading a burro behind him. She went to the gate to welcome the man. He looked at her long and seriously and then said, "You must be Mareth." Mareth asked what she could do for him. The man's face was sad and tired. "I have searched for you a long time," he continued. "I was sent by my Master to find you. Years and years ago you gave Him this burro. You gave her to Him when He was a tiny baby lying in your father's stable. He was told how you loved her, how tears stood in your eyes when you parted with her. He has taken good care of her. He, too, loved her. He will need her no longer, and He asked that I find you and return her."

Mareth looked down at the burro. Again her eyes filled with tears. Of course — it was Tallah, and Tallah seemed to recognize her, too. Mareth threw her arms around Tallah's dusty neck. Her tears fell on Tallah's face, still gentle, still beautiful, with the same soft eyes.

"And now I must be on my way," the man said. "My name is Peter. I have a long way to go still and much work to do." As he turned to leave, he paused for a moment and stood gazing at Mareth, filled with joy to have Tallah back, Tallah standing still and quiet as if she knew this was her home now and there would be no more wandering.

Mareth stroked Tallah's ears, her head, her back, and then suddenly stopped in amazement and wonder. "But look!" she cried. "Look! Tallah has a new marking across her shoulders and down her back!" And she traced the marking with her fingers. It was true — there was a black cross which reached across her shoulders and down her back to the tip of her tail. "Look!" Mareth continued. "She wears a cross on her back." She looked at Peter in astonishment, and Peter nodded and said, "Yes. This burro went everywhere with my Master, and her back was smooth and gray with never a mark on it. No mark at all, until one day she carried my Master on her back into the city of Jerusalem and people spread palms along the way for Tallah to walk on as she bore my Master. Ever since then," Peter continued, "Tallah has worn this mark. I have never seen another burrow who had it, but perhaps from now on all burros will wear it, and it will be a reminder always that it was a burro who carried my Master on that day of palms."

And with no other word, Peter turned and disappeared down the road. Mareth looked after him until he was out of sight. Then she turned to Tallah,

hugged her once again, and led her to the pasture where the other animals were. There were tall, sweet grasses there, there was a cool brook running near. And this is where Tallah stayed, surrounded by love and good care, for the rest of her long and happy life.